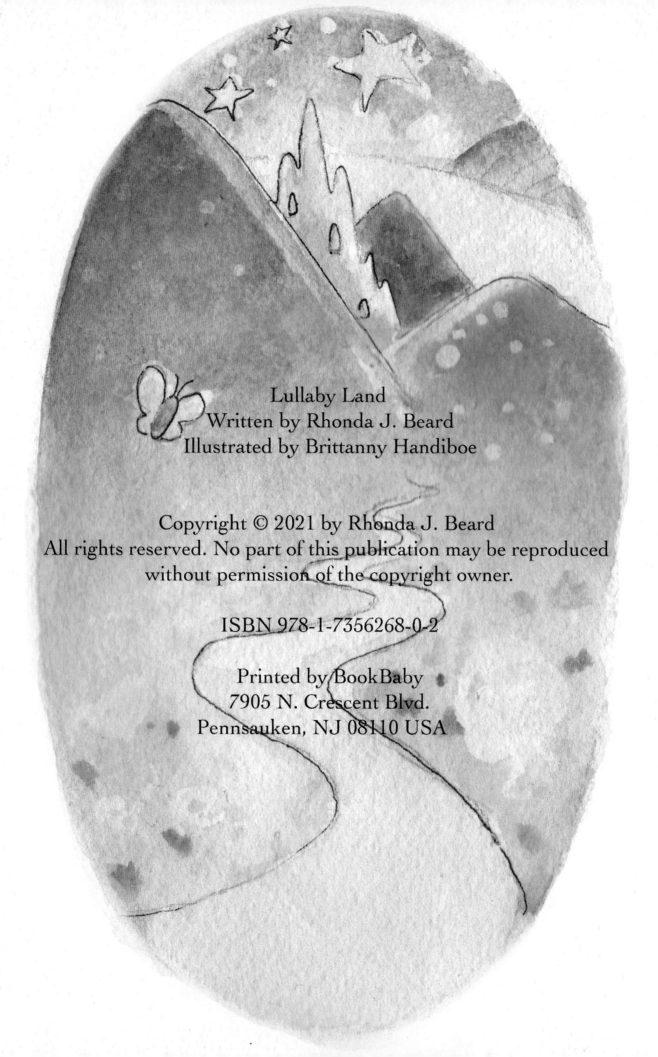

Lullaby Land
Written by Rhonda J. Beard
Illustrated by Brittanny Handiboe

ISBN 978-1-7356268-0-2

Printed by BookBaby
7905 N. Crescent Blvd.
Pennsauken, NJ 08110 USA

To my husband Rod,

Thank you so much for all
of your encouragment and support!
I love you always,
Rhonda.

Lullaby Land
was inspired by and is dedicated to
my children; Brindsay, Bretton, and Brogan.
I love yous',
MoM

Lullaby Land

Words by Rhonda J. Beard
Pictures by Brittanny Handiboe

Welcome to Lullaby Land...

a wonderland of dreams.

Where everything, here or there,
is as it seems.

Just close your eyes
when it's time to sleep.

Sweet dreams are yours
to mindfully keep.

Come with me to Lullaby Land.

I'll lead the way
just take my hand.

Come inside to stay and play
for an hour or all day.

You may stay
how long you choose,

for a short
or longer snooze.

Never sadness, crying,
pouting or frowns

because we turn frowns
up side down!

To smiles, laughter,
giggles, and grins,

In Lullaby Land,
happiness begins.

We see smiling faces
and grins from ear-to-ear,

Laughs and giggles
and smiley-eyely tears.

There's sunshine and rainbows
and white puffy clouds.

The sun shines so brightly-
it's nearly out loud!

Songbirds are singing
every which where,

And butterflies flutterby
here and there.

The leaves are
dancing in the trees.

And honey makes music
with the bees.

Flowers are bursting
forth in bloom

This is Lullaby
Land's heirloom!

The rainbows last forever
in Lullaby Land.

The sight is so awesome
it's wonderfully grand.

On white puffy clouds
it's the best way to roam.

To Lullaby Land
and then on back home.

As in the real world
some raindrops must fall.

In Lullaby Land,
they're not like raindrops at all.

The drops are the color
of the rainbow within.

The colors are brilliant
from beginning to end!

There are RED drops and BLUE
drops and YELLOW and GREEN.

ORANGE drops, PURPLE drops
all shades in between.

Close your eyes and follow me
Come to Lullaby Land and see,

All the wonderous dreams perceive
will come true-

If you believe.

An enchanted wonder-land
of fun and joy,

Lullaby Land is for
EVERY girl and boy!

We sing lullabies
all day through,

Some that are old,
and some that are new.

Together we'll stroll
on by and by.

We'll ponder the ocean
and gaze at the sky.

It's never night-
only daylight with stars.

Their bright twinkling light
to behold is ours.

Lullaby Land is a wonder-land
of dreams come true,

A land that is wonderfully grand-

Just for you.

Where dreams never end
until you awake.

And you're back in your bed
for happiness sake.

So remember child

Just close your eyes
when it's time to sleep.

Sweet dreams are yours
to mindfully keep.

HUSH...

for off you'll be in a
land far away.

to Lullaby Land,

forever and a day.

Rhonda J. Beard
grew up in a small
rural town in central
Pennsylvania. As long as she can
remember, she loved poetry.
The great outdoors, animals, and
nature were all around which inspired
her to write poetry, stories, and
rhymes. Becoming a Wife, Mother,
and then a Nana provided more inspiration
and more to write about!

Brittanny Handiboe was born
and raised just south of Baltimore Maryland.
She doodled in her picture books as a
child because her dream was to simply
add her own pictures to the words.
That dream hasn't changed much
besides, well, doodling
in other picture books...
sorry Dr. Seuss.